Great Expectations

Great Expectations

by
Charles Dickens

Adapted by
Nicole Vittiglio

Illustrated by
Michael Jaroszko

Modern Publishing
A Division of Unisystems, Inc.
New York, New York 10022

Series UPC: 39305

Cover art by Marcel Laverdet

Contents

CHAPTER 1

The Convict on the Marshes

My last name is Pirrip, and my first name is Philip. When I was very young, I could pronounce nothing more than Pip. So I came to be known as Pip.

My mother and father died when I was a baby. I never saw them, for this was long before the days of photographs. I was raised by my sister, Mrs. Joe Gargery, and her husband.

We lived in the marsh country, down by the river. I spent hours in the churchyard where my parents were buried. During one visit, after darkness fell, I became frightened. The wind rushed in, and the sea was very rough. I shivered and began to cry.

"Hold your noise!" cried a terrible voice. A man rose from among the graves at the side of the church porch. "Keep still or I'll cut your throat!"

He was dressed all in gray with a rag tied around his head. A leg iron made of metal rings with a ball and chain attached was fastened around one of his legs. His shoes were falling apart, and he was smeared with mud. He walked with a limp, and his teeth chattered.

"Don't cut my throat, sir," I pleaded.

"Tell me your name!" said the man.

"Pip, sir," I said.

"Show me where you live," he said.

I pointed to our village, about a mile from the church. The man looked at me for a moment, then turned me upside down and emptied my pockets. All I had was a piece of bread. The man grabbed it and ate ravenously.

"Where's your mother?" he asked.

I pointed to the graves.

"Who do you live with, then?" he asked. "That is, supposin' I decide to let you live."

"My sister, sir. Mrs. Joe Gargery, wife of the blacksmith," I said.

"Blacksmith, eh?" he said. He looked at his leg for some time, then grabbed me by both arms and tilted me back as far as he could. "Do you know what a file is?" he asked.

"Yes, sir," I replied.

"And do you know what food is?" he asked.

"Yes, sir," I replied again.

"Well, get a file and some food and bring 'em to me," he ordered, "at that old Battery over yonder, very early in the morning. If you do it without saying a word to anyone, I'll let you live. If not, I'll tear your heart out. And I ain't alone. There's a man over yonder who is an angel compared with me."

I nodded and ran toward home.

CHAPTER 2

A Robbery

My sister was more than twenty years older than I was. She had a great reputation with the neighbors because she had brought me up "by hand." She had a very heavy hand. I guess that Joe and I were both brought up "by hand."

My sister was not a good-looking woman, and she was mean. Joe was a kind, good-natured fellow. I thought that Mrs. Joe must have made Joe marry her "by hand."

Joe's forge adjoined our house. When I arrived home from the churchyard, the forge was shut. Joe sat alone in the kitchen.

"Mrs. Joe is out looking for you," he

said. "She's got Tickler with her."

This was dismal news. Tickler was a wax-ended piece of cane, worn smooth by collision with my body.

"I hear her coming now," Joe said. "Hurry up and hide behind the door."

I took his advice. My sister threw the door wide open. Finding an obstruction behind it, she poked Tickler in to investigate. Then she threw me at Joe.

"Where have you been, you young monkey?" she asked, stamping her foot.

"To the churchyard," I said, crying.

"If it weren't for me, you'd be in the churchyard by now," she said. "Who brought you up by hand?"

"You did," I said.

"Why I did it, I don't know," she said. "It's bad enough to be a blacksmith's wife without having to be your mother."

The fugitive out on the marshes, the mysterious young man, the file, the food, and the dreadful promise I had made were heavy on my mind.

My sister buttered some bread for us. Although I was hungry, I felt that I must save it for the man with the leg iron. I knew that Mrs. Joe kept a close eye on the food in the house. I put my bread down the leg of my trousers.

Since it was Christmas Eve, my sister was busier than usual. She ordered me to stir the pudding for the next day. After I had stirred for an hour, I sat by the fireplace to warm myself before being sent off to bed. Suddenly, I heard guns being fired.

"There's another convict off," Joe said, shaking his head.

"What do you mean, Joe?" I asked.

Mrs. Joe always took it upon herself to explain things. She said, snappishly, "Escaped. Escaped."

"Where does the firing come from?" I asked.

Joe tried to save me by mouthing the answer, but I could not tell what he was saying. So I asked her again.

"From the hulks," she snapped.

"And what's the hulks?" I asked.

"Answer one question, and he'll ask you a dozen more," my sister huffed. "Hulks are the prison ships right across the marshes."

Mrs. Joe hit me on the side of my head with her thimble. She told me that people were put on the prison ships for asking too many questions.

As I walked up the steps to bed, I felt sure that I was on my way to the hulks. I

had begun by asking questions, and I soon was going to rob Mrs. Joe. I was in mortal terror of the man with the bound leg. I was in mortal terror of the promise I had made. I had no hope!

Very early the next morning, I went downstairs. The pantry was well stocked. I stole some bread, cheese, half of a jar of mincemeat, a meat bone with very little on it, and a pork pie.

I unlocked a door in the kitchen that led to the forge. I got a file from among Joe's tools. Then I ran for the misty marshes.

CHAPTER 3
Captured!

The mist was heavy when I got out on the marshes, so that instead of my running toward everything, everything seemed to rush up to me. In my mind, I could hear people accusing me of being a thief.

Finally, I reached the Battery. The man was sitting in front of me, sleeping. I walked up to him and touched him gently on the shoulder. He jumped up, but it was not the same man! He was dressed exactly the same way as the first man. He had the exact same limp. He swung at me, but missed. Then he ran off into the mist.

The first man came limping toward

me. He shivered from the cold. I handed him the sack of food, and he shoved the food down his throat. Then he turned as though he had heard a sound in the distance.

"You brought no one with you?" he asked suspiciously.

"No, sir! No!" I cried.

"Well," he said, "I believe you."

"I am afraid there will be no food left for him," I said. "There's no more to be gotten where that came from."

"Who's him?" he asked.

"The man you mentioned before," I replied nervously.

"He don't want no vittles!" he returned, with a gruff laugh.

"He looked as if he did," I said.

The man stopped eating. "Looked? When?" he asked.

"Just now," I answered. I told him that the man was wearing a leg iron just like his and told him about the cannon that we heard the night before.

He said that he hadn't heard it from his spot on the marshes.

He asked me about the other man. I reported that he had a bruise on his face. My new friend seemed to know the exact spot.

He started off after the other man, but then stopped. He dropped down and began to file his leg iron fiercely, despite the bleeding cut he was filing against. I told him I must go.

Since he took no notice, I slipped off.

The last I saw of him, he was bent over his knee, filing.

When I returned home, I expected to find the police waiting for me. But Mrs. Joe was busy getting the house ready for the holiday festivities. Joe had been sent out to the kitchen doorstep.

"And where have you been?" Mrs. Joe scolded. I told her I had been down to see the carolers.

"If I wasn't slaving away here, maybe I could have gone to hear the carols," said Mrs. Joe.

Joe came into the kitchen. When Mrs. Joe looked away, he secretly crossed his two forefingers. That was our secret sign that Mrs. Joe was cross. This was so often her normal state that Joe and I used the sign a lot.

Mr. Wopsle, the clerk at church, was to dine with us, as were Mr. Hubble and Mrs. Hubble. Joe's Uncle Pumblechook was also coming. Mrs. Joe treated him as if he were her own uncle. Uncle

Pumblechook was well-to-do and drove his own carriage. I was not allowed to call him uncle.

Mr. Wopsle arrived first, followed by the Hubbles. Pumblechook arrived last. He was a large man, with a mouth like a fish and dull, staring eyes.

As he did every Christmas, Uncle Pumblechook said, "Mrs. Joe, I have brought something, as the compliments of the season," presenting her with two desserts. He brought the same thing every Christmas and announced it in the same way.

And Mrs. Joe always replied in the same way, too. "Oh, Un-cle Pum-ble-chook, you are so kind," she gushed.

We dined in the kitchen. Then we went into the parlor for dessert. My sister was unusually gracious in the presence of company.

I was squeezed in at the corner of the table, with the table pressed against

my chest. Pumblechook's elbow was in my eye.

Mr. Wopsle told me that we must truly be grateful for all we had. My sister repeated his words. Pumblechook told me that I should be especially grateful to those who brought me up by hand.

Everyone thought that I was an ungrateful boy who would amount to no good. Mrs. Hubble said that I caused my sister a lot of trouble. Mrs. Joe agreed wholeheartedly.

My sister treated Joe even more harshly when there was company, but he was always polite and helpful. He always made sure that I had gravy, if there was any, with dinner.

"Would you like some pork pie, Uncle?" my sister asked.

Now Mrs. Joe would discover my thievery! When she went out to get the pie, Mr. Hubble remarked that a bit of pork pie would be lovely. Joe told me that I could have a big piece. I could not bear any more. I got up and ran.

When I got to the door, I ran right into a group of policemen. One held out a pair of handcuffs, saying, "Here you are, come on!"

The sight of policemen with guns caused everyone at the table to rise in confusion. Just then, Mrs. Joe entered the kitchen empty-handed.

"Excuse me, ladies and gentlemen," said the sergeant. "I am here in the name of the king. The blacksmith's services are required."

"And what might you want with him?" my sister asked.

"The lock is broken on these hand-cuffs. We would like you to fix them," the sergeant said.

Joe looked at them. The job required him to light his forge fire. So he told the officers that the job would take at least two hours. The sergeant and his men piled their arms in a corner of the kitchen.

I watched without realizing fully what was going on. I wondered if they had come to arrest me.

"How far are the marshes from here?" the sergeant asked.

"Just a mile," Mrs. Joe said.

"Are you after convicts?" Mr. Wopsle asked, interrupting.

"Yes," the sergeant replied. "There are two of them. Have any of you seen such men?"

Everybody, except me, said no. While

Joe and some of the policemen worked in the forge, my sister offered tea and dessert to the other officers.

At last Joe finished. He suggested that some of us go with the officers to help. Pumblechook and Mr. Hubble declined, but Mr. Wopsle offered to go. Joe said that he would take me along. I am sure that Mrs. Joe would never have allowed it, but she was curious to know what would happen.

So we set off, the officers in front and Joe, Mr. Wopsle, and me in the rear. I was afraid that, if we found them, my convict would think that I had betrayed him to the police.

With my heart thumping, I looked for signs of the convicts. Suddenly, the officers stopped in their tracks. We heard a shout. A few minutes later, we heard it again. The sergeant ordered us to be silent and change direction to follow the sounds.

At the sergeant's orders, we ran up

and down banks, over gates, and into bushes. As we got closer, we could hear more than one voice calling, "Murder!" "Convicts!" and "Runaways!"

"Here are both men," shouted the sergeant. "Surrender, you two!"

A few of the officers ran down into a ditch to capture the convicts. There was a struggle, some splashing, and much mud flying around in the bottom of the ditch. Finally, the soldiers dragged the two convicts out.

"He tried to murder me," the other convict said. "I'd have been a dead man if you hadn't arrived."

"I dragged him back here and stopped him from escapin'," my convict said. "I did you a favor, Sergeant."

The sergeant ordered his officers to light their torches. My convict spotted me for the first time. I shook my head and moved my hands in a way to show that I had not given him up.

Then we all marched out of the

marshes. We came to a wooden hut, where a guard was waiting for the convicts. He recorded their names, and the other convict was led away to the prison ship.

"I want to say something," my convict said. "While I was out in the marshes, I had some vittles from the blacksmith's house."

The sergeant looked at Joe. Then Joe turned to me. Both Joe and the officers thought that the convict stole the food.

They didn't suspect me. My convict thanked Joe for the food.

"Well, we don't know what you're guilty of," said Joe, "but we wouldn't want you to starve to death for it."

My convict was led onto the prison ship. Then the ship sailed away into the dark night.

I knew that I should have told Joe the truth about stealing his file and the pie, but I didn't. I was afraid that Joe would think badly of me. I loved him too much for that to happen.

When we finally got home, Joe told them all about my convict's confession. All of our visitors suggested different ways by which he had gotten into the pantry. Pumblechook thought that he had gone from the roof of the forge to the roof of the house, and had crawled down the kitchen chimney.

That was the last thing I heard before my sister ordered me off to bed.

CHAPTER 4
An Offer for Pip

Until I was old enough to be apprenticed to Joe, I did odd jobs around the forge. If any neighbor needed some help picking up stones or cleaning their yard, I was given the job. My sister kept a box on the mantel, into which I had to drop all of my earnings. I was not allowed to keep any.

I went to a school in the village, run by Mr. Wopsle's great-aunt. She was very old and had the habit of falling asleep during class. Mr. Wopsle rented the room upstairs. Often, the students could hear him reading aloud.

His great-aunt had a general store in the schoolroom. She had no idea what she had in stock, or any of the prices. Biddy, her granddaughter, ran the shop.

Like me, Biddy was an orphan. She was brought up by hand, as well. Her hair needed brushing, and her hands were always dirty.

Biddy was kind to me and undertook my education. Slowly, I began to read and write a little.

One night, about a year after our convict hunt, I sat down to write a letter to Joe, who was learning to read along with me. I struggled and finally finished the letter, which was written in very poor English and with many misspellings. Joe read it carefully.

"You're quite the scholar, ain't you?" Joe asked. Joe was uneducated and could hardly read.

"Why didn't you go to school?" I asked him.

Joe explained that his father had been very mean. Several times he and his mother had tried to run away, but

his father would always find them. Then they would have to go back home. Joe would have to leave the school he was in at the time. His father died suddenly, so then Joe had to work to help his mother. Soon after his mother died, Joe met my sister and me.

"No matter what anyone thinks, your sister is a fine woman," Joe said.

I didn't agree, but I didn't want to say so. I replied, "I'm glad you think so."

"We're the best of friends, ain't we,

Pip?" Joe asked. I agreed and hugged him tightly.

"Pip, I like these reading lessons of ours," Joe said. "But your sister must never find out. She likes to be in charge of us and she thinks that if I get too smart, I might rebel."

I wanted to ask why Joe didn't take charge and rebel, but he stopped me. Joe said that Mrs. Joe was very smart and he wasn't. He said he would never mistreat his wife like his father had done. I had a new admiration for Joe after that night.

Just then, we heard Pumblechook's carriage coming up the road. Mrs. Joe had gone to the market with Pumblechook to help with things that required a woman's opinion. Joe and I set out a chair for Mrs. Joe, stirred the fire, and made sure that everything in the kitchen was in place.

"Now," said Mrs. Joe, "if this boy ain't grateful tonight, he never will be!"

I looked as grateful as I could, even though I didn't know what I should be grateful for. I looked at Joe, but he had no idea what was going on.

"Miss Havisham wants this boy to play at her house," Mrs. Joe said.

Everyone we knew had heard of Miss Havisham. She was a very rich lady who lived in a large, gloomy house. She led a very secluded life.

"How does she know Pip?" Joe asked.

"Who said she knew him?" my sister

shouted. "Uncle Pumblechook is her tenant. She asked him if he knew of any little boys to go and play there."

I was to stay at Pumblechook's apartment and he would take me to Miss Havisham in the morning. My sister scrubbed me until I was clean. Then she dressed me in my stiffest suit and delivered me to Pumblechook.

I had never parted from Joe before. "Good-bye, Joe!" I cried.

"Good-bye, Pip, old chap!" Joe replied.

CHAPTER 5

Satis House

The next morning, Pumblechook took me to Miss Havisham's house. It was old brick and had many iron bars on it. Some of the windows had been covered over. The ones that weren't had rusty bars across them.

After ringing the bell, we waited in the courtyard for someone to open the door. Finally a young lady came across the courtyard with keys in her hand.

"This," said Pumblechook, "is Pip."

"Come in, Pip," the girl said. She was very pretty and seemed very proud.

Pumblechook was about to walk in with us, but the girl stopped him. She assured him that Miss Havisham did not wish to see him. He looked at me as though I had done something wrong. He told me to behave myself.

The girl led me across the courtyard. The wind seemed to be much colder there. The girl told me that her name was Estella and the name of the place was Satis House. Satis, she said, meant "enough."

"Don't loiter, boy," the girl said. She kept calling me "boy." She said it in a very mean way. She was about my age,

but seemed much older.

We entered the house through a side door. Inside, there were many passages, and it was very dark. The girl picked up a candle and led me down one of the passages and up a staircase.

At last we came to the door of a room, and she said, "Go in."

"After you, miss," I said shyly.

"Don't be ridiculous. I'm not going in," she said. Then she walked away.

I was uncomfortable and afraid, but I knocked on the door. A voice inside told me to enter. The room was large and well lit with candles. There was not a bit of daylight in the room.

The strangest lady I had ever seen sat in a chair. She wore white satin, lace, and silk. She had a long white veil. Bridal flowers decorated her white hair. All of the white things had yellowed from age. Some bright jewels sparkled on her neck and on her hands, and some other jewels lay on the table beside her.

Dresses, less splendid than the dress she wore, and half-packed trunks, were scattered about. She had not finished dressing, for she had on only one shoe. I saw that the dress had been meant for the figure of a young woman, but the figure upon which it now hung had shrunk to skin and bone. A clock in the room had stopped at twenty minutes to nine.

"Who is it?" the lady asked.

"Pip, ma'am," I said.

"Come nearer. Let me look at you," she said. She touched my heart and cried, "Broken!" She said it with a weird smile on her face.

Then she ordered me to play. I had a fear of what my sister would do to me if she found out that I had refused to play. But, at that moment, I could not bring myself to start playing.

"Call Estella," Miss Havisham said. I did as I was told.

Finally Estella came into the room. Miss Havisham told her that all of the

jewels would be hers one day. Then she told Estella to play cards with me.

"He is such a common boy!" Estella complained.

"So you can break his heart," Miss Havisham answered.

I began to realize that everything in the room had stopped a long time ago, just like the clock. Miss Havisham watched us as we played cards.

"This boy has such rough hands," Estella said in disgust. I had never been ashamed of my hands before.

I dealt the cards the wrong way, and Estella called me stupid.

"You say nothing back to her," Miss Havisham warned. "She may say hard things of you, but you say nothing of her. What do you think of her?"

"I don't want to say," I stammered.

"Tell me in my ear," she said.

"I think she is very proud and very pretty," I whispered.

"Anything else?" Miss Havisham demanded.

"I think she is very rude," I said.

"Anything else?" Miss Havisham asked again.

"I would like to go home," I said.

"You shall go soon," said Miss Havisham. "Finish the game."

When Estella had beaten me at cards for the final time, Miss Havisham said, "Come again after six days."

"Yes, ma'am," I said.

Estella led me outside. "You are to

wait here, boy," she said. She disappeared and closed the door.

For the first time in my life, I wished Joe's upbringing had been more genteel. Then I would have been, too.

Estella came back with some food and drink for me. She put it on the floor, as she would have for a dog. I was so humiliated and angry that I began to cry. She looked delighted.

Estella went to get the keys to let me out. When she came back she asked me why I wasn't crying anymore.

"Because I don't want to," I said.

"You do," she said. "You have been crying until you are half blind. Now you are near crying again." She laughed, pushed me out, and locked the gate.

CHAPTER 6

An Unexpected Stranger

When I got home, my sister wanted to know all about Miss Havisham's home. Before long, she was shoving me because my answers were not good enough. I was sure that if I described it as I had seen it, I would not be understood. So I said as little as I could, and had my face shoved against the kitchen wall.

Old Pumblechook approached to find out the details.

"How did it go, boy?" he said.

"Pretty well, sir."

"Boy! What is Miss Havisham like?" Pumblechook asked.

I said that Miss Havisham sat on a black velvet couch, and that Estella served us cake on gold plates. My story continued with four giant dogs fighting over veal cutlets in a silver basket.

They looked at each other in amazement. When Joe came in from the forge, my sister repeated the story. Then she and Pumblechook discussed what kind of reward I might get from Miss Havisham.

When I saw the look of wonder on Joe's face, I felt guilty for telling tales. I didn't care what the others thought, but I didn't want to be a monster to Joe. So I told him the truth when we were alone.

I also told Joe about how pretty Estella was, and how mean she had been. I told him that I wished I were not so common.

"You are uncommon in some ways," Joe said. "You are uncommonly small and you are an uncommon scholar."

"I am ignorant and backward," I said dismally.

"Even the king had to begin at A

before he could get to Z," Joe said.

There was some hope in this piece of wisdom. Yet, when I was alone in my little room, it hurt to think what Estella would think of Joe.

A few days later, I decided to ask Biddy to help me by teaching me everything she knew. She promised that she would.

One evening, Biddy gave me an old dictionary to copy. On my way home, I was to stop at the public house and get Joe. Those were my sister's orders.

I found Joe sitting with Mr. Wopsle and a stranger. I sat down next to Joe.

"So, you're the blacksmith," the stranger said to Joe.

Joe introduced Mr. Wopsle as the church clerk. The man knew exactly where the church was located along the marshes. He even knew about the graveyard.

"Do you ever see any tramps out in the marshes?" the stranger asked.

"Only an escaped convict every now and again," Joe answered, mentioning the night we chased the convicts.

The strange man looked at only me. It made me uncomfortable. The man stirred his drink with a file. He did this so that nobody but me saw the file. It was Joe's file. Could it be that this man knew my convict?

As Joe and I were about to leave, the stranger stopped us.

"If I've got a shilling in my pocket, the

boy shall have it," the stranger said. He found the shilling, folded it in some crumpled paper, and gave it to me.

My sister was not in a very bad temper when we came in, so Joe told her about the shilling. When she grabbed the shilling, the crumpled papers—two one-pound notes!—fell to the ground.

Joe ran to the public house to return the money to the stranger, but he was already gone. My sister folded up the money and put it in the cupboard.

CHAPTER 7

A Pale Young Gentleman

The next Wednesday, I returned to Miss Havisham's. Once again, Estella locked the gate after letting me in. Ignoring me, she led me through a different passage.

At the end of the passage, we went through a door that led to another courtyard. At the other end, a clock hung on the wall. It had stopped at twenty minutes to nine.

Then Estella showed me into a gloomy room with a low ceiling.

"Stand there until you are wanted, boy," Estella said, pointing to a window.

Three ladies and a gentleman were in the room, talking about a man named

Matthew. Then a bell rang in the distance.

Estella came back into the room. "Now, boy," she ordered. I followed her out into the hallway.

As we were walking, Estella turned suddenly and stuck her face right up against mine. "Am I pretty?" she asked.

"Yes. You are very pretty," I replied.

She slapped my face quite hard. "What do you think of me now, you little animal?" she asked.

"I shall not tell you," I answered.

"Why don't you go ahead and cry again?" Estella asked.

"I'll never cry for you again," I said. But I was crying on the inside.

On our way upstairs, we ran into a large man. He took my chin in his hands and warned me to behave myself. Then, without another word, he walked away.

Everything in Miss Havisham's room was exactly as it was the first time I was there.

"Are you ready to play?" Miss Havisham asked. She instructed me to wait for her in a room across the hall.

This room was dark and dusty. Cobwebs covered everything. I watched some beetles play in the corner until Miss Havisham grabbed my shoulder.

"This," she said, pointing to a long table, "is where I will be laid when I am dead. Do you know what that is under those cobwebs? It is my wedding cake."

She leaned on my shoulder and

ordered me to walk her around the room. After quite a while, she called for Estella. Estella brought with her the company from downstairs.

"Dear Miss Havisham," said one of the ladies, whose name was Miss Sarah Pocket. "How well you look!"

"I do not," Miss Havisham retorted. "I am yellow skin and bone."

The discussion returned to Matthew. They noted how sad it was that he never visited Miss Havisham. Then they bid Miss Havisham farewell and were led out by Estella.

"Today is my birthday, Pip," Miss Havisham said. I was going to wish her a happy birthday, but she spoke again.

"When I die and they lay me out in my bridal gown, the curse will be upon him!" she growled. I said nothing, but just stood and stared at her.

Finally, Miss Havisham told me to play cards with Estella. When we were done, Miss Havisham appointed a day

for my return, and Estella coldly led me out. In the courtyard, a pale young man said hello.

"Who let you in?" he asked.

"Estella did," I said.

"Come and fight," he ordered. He slapped my head and rammed his head into my stomach. I hit him back. He dodged while I looked helplessly at him. I was afraid of him. He was about my age, but much taller.

He insisted that we have a boxing

match. To my suprise, I won. He seemed so brave that I felt bad about my victory. We said good-bye and parted.

Back in the courtyard, Estella was waiting to let me out. She looked delighted.

"You may kiss me," she said.

I kissed her cheek as she turned it to me. I felt that she had allowed the kiss to me as a coin might have been given to a beggar. It was worth nothing.

CHAPTER 8

Joe's Apprentice

For many days I stayed close to home. I was afraid that the pale young man would find me and make me pay for winning the boxing match.

My terrors reached a new height when it was time for me to go back to Miss Havisham's.

I imagined all kinds of things, but nothing happened. The fight was not mentioned. The pale young man was nowhere to be seen.

On every visit to Miss Havisham's, she insisted that I push her around the room in a wheelchair. She asked me questions. I told her that I was to be apprenticed to Joe, but that I was eager to learn new things. She seemed to prefer that I remain ignorant.

Estella never asked me to kiss her again. Sometimes she seemed to hate me, sometimes to like me. Miss Havisham watched us play cards. Often I could hear her whisper to Estella, "Break their hearts and show no mercy!"

I discussed Miss Havisham and Estella with no one but Biddy. I trusted her. She was smart and understood things. I knew that Biddy had a deep concern for me.

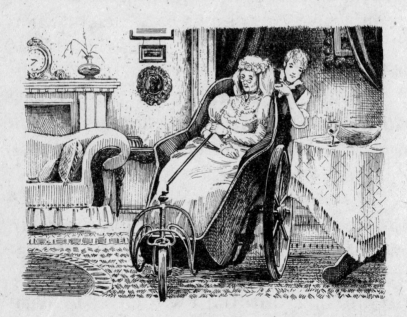

Pumblechook frequently dined with us. When he did, he and my sister would have a long discussion about Miss Havisham.

One day, Miss Havisham remarked that I was getting tall. By this time, I was old enough to be apprenticed to Joe. She asked me to bring Joe to the house to meet her.

When I told my sister that Miss Havisham wished to meet Joe, Mrs. Joe yelled and threw things. She was jealous of poor Joe.

When the day arrived to visit Miss Havisham, Joe dressed in his finest suit. I thought he looked better in his work clothes, but I did not tell him so. He seemed very uncomfortable in his suit.

My sister insisted on coming to town with us. She was going to spend the afternoon at Pumblechook's house. We left her there and hurried on to Miss Havisham's.

Estella let us in. When we went into

her room, Miss Havisham looked up and asked about my apprenticeship. Poor Joe just stood there with his mouth open, shocked by what he saw. He was afraid of her and looked at me when he answered. I am ashamed to say that he embarrassed me.

"Pip has earned a wage here," Miss Havisham said. "There are twenty-five pounds in this bag. Give it to your master, Pip."

Joe thanked me kindly instead of thanking Miss Havisham.

"Good-bye, Pip!" said Miss Havisham. "Let them out, Estella."

"Am I to come again, Miss Havisham?" I asked.

"No. The blacksmith is your master now," she replied.

Estella led us out, and we went back to Pumblechook's. Mrs. Joe demanded a report. Joe told her about the money that Miss Havisham had given him. My sister was quite pleased.

That day, I officially became Joe's apprentice. The thing that I remember most about that day was feeling that I would never be happy in Joe's trade. I had liked it once, but now things were different.

It is a terrible thing to be ashamed of one's home, but I hoped that Mrs. Havisham and Estella would never have a chance to see my home.

I now had new expectations. I wished to become a gentleman. I hated working in the forge with Joe, but I loved him and was loyal to him.

Soon I was too old to attend school, and Biddy had already taught me all that she knew. I tried to pass on to Joe what I had learned, but he didn't catch on very well. He was simple, and content with his life.

After I had been Joe's apprentice for almost a year, I decided to go back to Miss Havisham's for a visit. Joe was afraid that Miss Havisham would think that I was coming back for more money.

"I want to show Miss Estel—Havisham that I remember her," I stammered.

Joe agreed to give me a half-day off the next day. He insisted that I never ask to return there if I was not received cordially. I agreed.

Joe's other worker at the forge was named Orlick. He was big and strong, but also very mean. Orlick did not like me. When I was very young, he told me that a devil lived in the corner of the forge. This devil, he said, used young boys as kindling for the fire.

Orlick was angry that Joe had given me a half-day holiday. He talked Joe into giving him a holiday as well.

"You're a fool!" my sister said to Joe. "I wish I were his master."

"You'd be everyone's master if you could," Orlick yelled.

In defense of his wife, Joe got into a fistfight with Orlick, who was certainly no match for Joe.

I went upstairs to get dressed for my visit to Miss Havisham's house. When I came back down, Joe and Orlick were cleaning up the mess that they had made. The house was peaceful again. I left to pay my visit.

Although I had passed through Miss Havisham's gate many times, I was nervous. I felt that anything could happen in this strange place.

Miss Sarah Pocket, one of the women who had been at Satis House on Miss

Havisham's birthday, let me in. Estella was nowhere in sight. Miss Havisham was alone.

"Well?" Miss Havisham said. "I hope you want nothing. You'll get nothing."

"No, indeed, Miss Havisham," I said. "I only wanted you to know that I am doing very well in my apprenticeship. I am much obliged to you."

I looked for Estella. Miss Havisham said, "She's overseas, getting a lady's education. She's prettier than ever and is admired by all who meet her."

Before I could think of something to say, I was dismissed. When the gate closed behind me, I felt more dissatisfied than ever with my life.

As I walked home, I looked into the shop windows, thinking of the things I might buy if I were a gentleman. Just then, Mr. Wopsle walked up to me. He was on his way to Pumblechook's and invited me along. Since I didn't want to go home, I accepted the invitation.

At Pumblechook's, they discussed a book that I had not read. Pumblechook delighted in pointing out my ignorance.

On our way home, a heavy fog began to settle in. Mr. Wopsle and I spotted Orlick slouching under a tree. We all walked together. Moments later, we heard the sound of a cannon coming from the the direction of the hulks.

"Someone's escaped," Orlick said.

As we approached the village, a man ran up to us. "There's something wrong up at your place, Pip," he cried. "Run!"

As we ran, the man said that some-one had broken into our house while Joe was out. There had been a violent attack, supposedly by convicts.

We didn't stop running until we got to the house. The whole village was there. Joe was standing over my sister, who was lying unconscious on the floor.

It was strange to see her so still and silent. She no longer seemed threaten-ing. For once, I did not cower in her presence.

CHAPTER 9

An Attack on Mrs. Joe

Joe had been at the public house. Just before nine o' clock, my sister had been outside saying good night to a farmworker. Joe returned home just before ten o' clock and found her unconscious, lying on the ground.

Nothing was stolen from the house. Nothing had been destroyed in the kitchen. She had been hit with something blunt and heavy. A convict's leg iron was on the floor beside my sister. There seemed to have been no argument. The attacker came in silently and suddenly and attacked her from behind.

After examining it, Joe found that the iron had been filed some time ago.

At first, the officers thought the attacker was an escaped convict.

Naturally, I thought of my convict, but I could not accuse him. I believed the attacker was either Orlick or the strange man from the public house who had shown me the file.

Orlick had been seen around town by several people. Although my sister had fought with him, she had quarreled with countless other people as well.

As for the strange man, if he had come back to get his two one-pound notes, my sister had been prepared to return them.

It was horrible to think that I had provided the weapon by supplying the convicts with a file. I considered confessing to Joe. For months, I debated, but I did not confess.

My sister remained very ill. Her hearing and sight were greatly impaired. She had to carry around a slate and write out her thoughts. Since she was a poor speller and Joe was a poor reader, this proved very difficult. She needed much help moving about. But her temper greatly improved.

We had trouble finding a suitable attendant for her. Then Mr. Wopsle's great-aunt died, and Biddy came to live with us. She took care of Mrs. Joe.

Biddy had no trouble understanding my sister's slate messages. When my sister realized this, she instantly scribbled the same symbol that she had been trying to get Joe and me to understand. It looked like a hammer.

Biddy instantly understood the message and told Joe. "It's Orlick!" Biddy said. "Mrs. Joe can't remember his name. She can only identify him by the hammer."

We called Orlick in and told him the story. I fully expected Mrs. Joe to be angry with him. But she seemed pleased to see him. He seemed pleased to see her. After that, hardly a day passed

without Mrs. Joe drawing the hammer and Orlick coming in to stand before her. No one knew what to make of it.

Eventually, I got used to being an apprentice. It was a routine life, split between the village and the marshes.

I visited Miss Havisham on my birthday. Everything there was the same as before, and Estella was still gone. Visiting Miss Havisham on my birthday became a tradition. Every year she gave me some money.

Almost a year after she had come to live with us, I began to notice a change in Biddy. Her hair became bright and neat and her hands were always clean. She was not beautiful and she could never be like Estella, but she had very thoughtful eyes.

"Biddy, how do you manage to learn everything I learn and keep up with me?" I asked one night. "I study after my work is done in the forge. But I never see you study." I was becoming vain about my

knowledge. I spent all of my spare money on books.

"I suppose I catch it—like a cold," Biddy answered.

I didn't know what to say. Biddy was so humble. I felt ashamed. I was beginning to think that Biddy was a rather extraordinary girl. She learned things very quickly and still had time to run our household.

"You had no chance before you came here. Now look at how improved you are," I said.

"But I was your first teacher, wasn't I?" Biddy said as she sewed.

It occurred to me that I hadn't been grateful enough to Biddy. I asked her to take a walk on the marshes with me. Joe could watch my sister, for she was never to be left alone again. I decided to tell Biddy about my secret ambitions.

"I want to be a gentleman," I declared.

"Aren't you happy as you are?" Biddy asked.

"I am disgusted with my life and calling," I said, sighing.

"That's a pity," Biddy replied.

I told her that if I could settle for being a blacksmith, we would have led a good life. Perhaps Biddy and I would even have married one day.

"I would have been good enough for you, wouldn't I?" I asked her.

"I am not particular," she said.

I knew she meant well. I said I would never have known that I was so common if no one had ever told me.

Biddy turned suddenly to face me. "Who told you that you were common?" she asked. "That is neither true nor polite."

"The beautiful young lady at Miss Havisham's," I answered. "I want to change for her."

"To win her over or to spite her?" Biddy asked quietly. "If it is to spite her, you'd be better off not caring what she thinks. If it is to win her over, I do not

think that she is worth winning over."

I cried a bit, in my frustration. Biddy comforted me. She told me that she was glad that I had confided in her.

As we continued walking, I thought about how good Biddy was. She was never insulting. She didn't change her personality from day to day. I could trust and rely on her. She would have done anything for me. Why did I not like her more than Estella?

"I wish I could make myself fall in love with you," I said.

"But you never will," she said.

On our way across the churchyard, we ran into Orlick. He insisted on walking us home. Biddy whispered to me that she wished he wouldn't. I told him that we didn't need him to come with us, but he followed anyway.

Curious to find out if Biddy believed Orlick was responsible for my sister's attack, I asked why she didn't like him. She told me that he admired her and it made her uncomfortable. That made me angry. How dare he admire my Biddy!

"But it makes no difference to you," said Biddy calmly.

"No, Biddy, it makes no difference to me," I said. "But I don't like it and I don't approve of it." From that day on, I kept a close eye on Orlick.

CHAPTER 10
Pip's Farewell

One Saturday night, I sat at the public house with Joe and Mr. Wopsle. Mr. Wopsle read aloud from the newspaper about a much-discussed murder that had been committed. I noticed that a strange man was watching us.

The man pointed to Mr. Wopsle. "So you believe the man is guilty," the stranger said. "Well, in England, one is innocent until proven guilty." Then he asked if there was a blacksmith named Joe Gargery among us.

"That is me," Joe said.

"Is your apprentice here?" he asked.

"I am here!" I cried.

The stranger was the man I had met

years ago on the stairs at Miss Havisham's. He asked for a private meeting with Joe and me at our house.

When we got back to the house, the man told us that his name was Jaggers. He was a lawyer from London. He said he had come to us on behalf of someone else, but he could not reveal that person's identity.

"I am here to relieve you of Pip as your apprentice," he said to Joe. "You want nothing for letting him go, right?"

"I would never let anything stand in Pip's way," Joe replied.

"This young man has great expectations," Jaggers said. Joe and I gasped and looked at each other.

Jaggers told us that I was to inherit a great deal of property. The present owner of this property insisted that I be brought up as a gentleman. My dream had finally come true. I was sure that Miss Havisham was going to provide for my future!

Jaggers said that the name of my benefactor was to remain a secret until that person wished to reveal it. A sum of money had been supplied for my education. Jaggers was to be my guardian.

"Mr. Matthew Pocket will be your tutor," Jaggers said. So this was the Matthew who had been spoken of at Miss Havisham's, I thought.

"You will see his son first," Jaggers said. "He lives in London."

I told him I would go immediately. He gave me money to buy new clothes before I left for London.

"Gargery, you look dumbfounded," Jaggers observed. "What if I could repay you for the loss of Pip's services?"

"Money could never make up for the loss of Pip," Joe said.

It hurt me to think that I was so excited to leave Joe. He was so good and so gentle. I told him that we would always be the best of friends.

Jaggers told me to get to London in a week's time. With that, he left.

Joe, Biddy, and my sister were sitting in the kitchen. Joe told Biddy my news. They both looked very sad, but congratulated me.

Biddy tried to convey the news to my sister, but she just nodded her head and laughed.

I never would have thought it possible, but I was rather gloomy. In some way, I was dissatisfied with myself.

"Joe, I think I shall have my new clothes sent to Mr. Pumblechook's," I said. "I don't want to be stared at by the people around here."

Joe argued that Mr. Wopsle and some others might want to see me in my new finery. But I agreed to show my new clothes only to Joe and Biddy on the night before I left.

I went up to my room. It made me strangely sad that I would not sleep here anymore. From my window, I watched as Biddy and Joe talked outside.

Morning brought a change in my attitude. Now I only felt sad that there were six days to get through before I could leave.

I took a walk through the church-yard to the marshes. While pondering whether Miss Havisham intended to better me for Estella, I fell asleep. When I woke up, Joe was beside me.

"You may be sure, dear Joe," I said, "that I shall never forget you. It is a pity, though, that you did not learn more during our lessons."

"I'm awfully dull, I know," Joe said. "I only know my trade."

When we got home, I asked Biddy to give Joe some lessons. This way, I would be able to offer him a position when I inherited my property.

Biddy seemed angry. "Have you ever considered that he may be too proud to let anyone take him away from a job that he does well?" she asked.

"I think you are jealous of my rise in fortune!" I said in a superior tone. I walked out of the room.

The next morning, I put on the best clothes I owned and went to see Mr. Trabb, the tailor.

"It may seem that I'm boasting," I said. "But I have inherited a large property." Mr. Trabb regarded me more highly once I had told him that. He showed me all of his finest fabrics. He measured me, and when he was

finished, he arranged to have my new clothes delivered to Pumblechook's.

Next I went to the hatter and the shoemaker. When my new wardrobe was complete, I ordered my ticket for the Saturday coach to London. Then I headed to Pumblechook's.

"My dear friend," Pumblechook said. "Congratulations on your new fortune! How deserving you are!"

Pumblechook seemed to want to be my best friend. He offered me the best food and drink that he had. He told me that he hoped my sister had meant well by raising me by hand. I could see him waving from his doorway when I was already blocks away.

Finally, Friday arrived. I went to Pumblechook's to try on my new clothes. Then I decided to go to Miss Havisham's to pay her a final visit.

She said, "Well, Pip?"

"I am going to London tomorrow," I said. "I have come into good fortune since I saw you last. I am so grateful for it, Miss Havisham!"

"So, you have been adopted by a rich person," Miss Havisham said.

"Yes," I replied.

"Not named," said Miss Havisham.

"No," I answered.

Miss Havisham seemed to be enjoying herself. Miss Sarah Pocket, who was also in the room, seemed quite jealous. She told me to abide by Jaggers and to be deserving of my new

fortune. Before I left, she held out her hand, and I bent down to kiss it.

As the evenings before my departure dwindled, I became more appreciative of Joe and Biddy. On the last evening, I dressed in my new clothes, much to their delight.

I was to leave for London at five the next morning. I told Joe that I wished to depart alone. I am ashamed to say that I did not want people to notice the difference between my fancy new clothes and Joe's old ones.

Biddy woke up very early to make me breakfast. After eating, I got up quickly. I kissed my sister, who just nodded and laughed, as usual. I kissed Biddy and hugged Joe. Then I left. When I looked back, Joe was crying and Biddy held her apron to her face.

I walked briskly through the village. I had spent my entire childhood there. Tears started to roll down my face.

I breathed more easily after I boarded the coach and was on my way, the world spread out before me.

CHAPTER 11
A New Beginning

The journey from my small town to the big city took five hours. At first glance, I found London to be rather crooked, narrow, and dirty.

When the coachman stopped the coach, I looked up and saw a gloomy street. The name JAGGERS was on a sign above the door. Mr. Jaggers was away from his office, but his clerk, Wemmick, let me in.

Mr. Jaggers's office was small and dismal. The only light in the room came from a small skylight. Many odd objects were scattered around the room—a rusty pistol, a sword, and several strange boxes and packages.

Jaggers's chair was made of black horsehair, with brass nails around it like a coffin.

It was awfully hot in the chamber, so I decided to take a walk while I waited for Mr. Jaggers to come back. I went down a street from which I could see the dome of St. Paul's from behind a grim stone building. This building was Newgate Prison. There were many dirty and ragged people standing around.

A very dirty minister of justice approached me. He asked if I would like to see a few trials. He could get me a front-row seat for a small fee. I declined, so he showed me the gallows and the place where criminals were whipped. He told me that four people were to be hanged the next day.

I stepped back into Jaggers's office, but he had not returned. By now, there were many more people waiting for him. They spoke well of Jaggers and gave me the impression that he was

quite a popular figure.

Finally, Jaggers came in. He didn't say anything to me. He addressed two other people first.

"Amelia, don't you know that you wouldn't be here if it weren't for me?"

"Oh, yes, sir," the woman said. "But I've come here about my Bill."

"Bill is in good hands," Jaggers replied. "If you bother me again about this, I'll drop the case. Have you paid Wemmick?"

The woman told him that she had paid. It seemed that was really all that Jaggers cared about. The woman left, not wishing to upset Jaggers any further.

Jaggers led me into his chamber. He said I was to go to Barnard's Inn to young Mr. Pocket's room. There was a bed waiting for me. Then we would go to visit Matthew Pocket, his father. Wemmick walked me to young Mr. Pocket's. On our way, we ran into many people going to see Jaggers. Wemmick told them that Jaggers wouldn't have a word with any of them.

After a long walk, we arrived at Barnard's Inn. The inn was a collection of shabby buildings squeezed together. Dilapidated curtains covered the cracked windows of the apartment. There were FOR RENT signs everywhere.

We went upstairs to young Mr. Pocket's rooms. A note on the door said he would return shortly.

Wemmick said good-bye. "As I keep the cash, we will most likely meet often," he said.

While I waited, I viewed the inn through a dirty window on the staircase. I decided that London was overrated. I wrote my name in the dirt on the window several times.

After almost an hour, a young man arrived. He was holding a paper bag in each arm.

"Mr. Pip?" he asked.

"Mr. Pocket?" I asked.

"I am sorry," he said. "I thought you would be arriving on the later coach. I've been out to Covent Garden Market to buy some food for your stay."

Mr. Pocket, Jr., led me through the door, saying that he would be happy to show me around London. His apartment was bare. He said that he earned his own keep and received no money from his father.

As I stood across from Mr. Pocket, I realized that he looked familiar.

"You're the boy I boxed at Miss Havisham's!" he said.

"And you," I replied, "are the pale young gentleman!"

We stood looking at each other until we both burst out laughing. We shook hands and agreed that the fighting was a thing of the past. Herbert (that was young Mr. Pocket's name) explained that Miss Havisham had invited him as she had done with me, but Herbert was

not to her liking.

"I suppose if I had met her expectations," Herbert said, "I might now be engaged to Estella."

"Are you disappointed?" I asked.

"No," Herbert answered. "Estella has been brought up by Miss Havisham to hate men." Herbert told me that Miss Havisham had adopted Estella.

Herbert also told me that Jaggers had suggested that his father, who was Miss Havisham's cousin, be my tutor.

Herbert was very easy to talk to. I could tell by looking at him that he was not secretive or mean. He was still a pale young gentleman, but he was quite cheerful, as well.

Herbert gave me the nickname Handel. He said that there was a charming piece of music by the composer Handel that was called the "Harmonious Blacksmith." I didn't know the piece, but I liked the nickname very much.

During dinner, Herbert revealed that Miss Havisham had been a spoiled child. Her mother died young. Her father owned a brewery and was rich. He married again, in secret, and Miss Havisham had a half-brother as a result of that union. Her half-brother was a bad seed, and the two did not get along. When their father died, Miss Havisham became an heiress and her half-brother inherited a lot of money.

Later, Miss Havisham met a man with whom she fell in love. This man claimed to be devoted to her. He got a lot of money from her, and he convinced her to buy out her half-brother's share of the brewery and let him manage it.

Herbert's father tried to warn her that she was doing too much for this man, but she would not listen. She ordered Herbert's father to leave her, and he had not seen her since that time.

On the day of her wedding, Miss Havisham received a cold-hearted letter from the groom, in which he said he

could not marry her. That was why all of the clocks in her house were stopped at twenty minutes to nine. Her half-brother and her fiancé were partners in the scheme. They split all of the money.

A few days later, we went to Mr. Pocket's house. Mrs. Pocket was reading in the garden. Herbert's young siblings were playing near her. Two nurses were trying to keep them quiet.

"Mama," said Herbert, "this is young Mr. Pip." She greeted me and then went back to her book.

Finally, Mr. Pocket came out. He had gray, messy hair, yet he was young looking. He had a confused expression on his face.

"Glad to meet you," Mr. Pocket said.

We went into the house and he showed me my room. Then he introduced me to his two other pupils. Bentley Drummle was a sulky, old-looking young man, the next heir to a baronetcy. The other man, intoduced to me merely as Startop, was younger in years and appearance.

CHAPTER 12

Dinner with Wemmick and Jaggers

After two or three days, I began to feel comfortable. Mr. Pocket said that Jaggers told him I was not yet intended for a particular profession. Until it was decided what I would do, Mr. Pocket would direct my studies.

Mr. Pocket was quite zealous in his teaching. In return, I was passionate about my studies. We had a good teacher-student relationship.

I knew I would be happy living with Herbert, so I asked Jaggers and Mr. Pocket, and they both consented. I was allowed to use some of the money from my benefactor to buy furniture.

Bentley Drummle was a sulky fellow.

He was heavy in figure, movement, and comprehension. He was idle, reserved, and suspicious. His wealthy family had encouraged these qualities in him.

Startop had been spoiled by a weak mother. He was kept at home, when he should have been in school. Naturally, I took much more kindly to Startop than I did to Drummle.

But Herbert was my best friend and companion. I let him share my rowboat, which was given to me by my benefactor. Herbert let me share his apartment.

I settled into my new surroundings and applied myself to my education. I soon picked up expensive habits and began to spend large amounts of money.

I hadn't seen Wemmick, Mr. Jagger's clerk, in a few weeks. One evening, I asked if I might visit his home. He agreed and asked me to meet him at the office.

"I hope you don't object to an aged

parent," Wemmick said apologetically when I met him. He had an elderly parent living with him.

"Mr. Jaggers told me that he will soon invite you to dinner," Wemmick informed me. "He's going to ask your pals, too. There are three, aren't there?"

Although I didn't consider Drummle as my pal, I answered, "Yes."

Wemmick's house was a little cottage in the middle of a garden. To get to it, we passed through lanes, ditches, and

gardens. Behind the cottage, was a castle with a drawbridge. That was where Wemmick really lived.

"I am my own carpenter and gardener," Wemmick said. "It's a good escape from city life. Would you mind meeting the Aged now?"

I said that I wouldn't, and we entered the house. A very old man sat by the fire. He was cheerful and seemed to be comfortable, but he was nearly deaf.

"How are you, aged parent?" Wemmick asked.

"All right, John," the old man replied.

We enjoyed a lovely dinner and nice conversation. I noted that Wemmick was lively and friendly when he was away from the office.

I stayed the night, and we had breakfast together in the morning. Then we walked back to Jaggers's office.

Just as Wemmick predicted, Jaggers invited my friends and me to dinner at his house. We met him at the office the

next evening. As we walked together, we encountered many people who wished to speak to Jaggers. He ignored all of them.

Jaggers's house was stately, but badly in need of painting. The windows were dirty. Jaggers led us into a bare, gloomy hall. As we sat down to dinner, I noticed that Jaggers was very possessive. He distributed everything himself.

This was the first time that Jaggers had met my friends. To my surprise, he seemed interested in Drummle only.

Jaggers's housekeeper served dinner. Whenever she was in the room, she did not take her eyes off of Jaggers.

Dinner went very well. By singling out Drummle, Jaggers caused Drummle to become quite full of himself. Drummle told the rest of us that we spent too much money. I told him that that was a funny remark coming from someone who had borrowed money from Startop the week before.

"You wouldn't lend any of us money," I noted.

"You're absolutely right," Drummle answered.

Herbert tried to get me to stop the argument, but to no avail. I told Drummle that I had observed that he was amused at Startop for being so weak as to lend him money. Drummle laughed and made it clear that he despised us all.

Startop made a witty remark to break the tension. Herbert and I laughed. Drummle resented Startop even more because of this. He was about to throw his glass across the room, but Jaggers stopped the fight.

We left Jaggers's house after this. Startop had already forgotten about the whole incident, but Drummle didn't. Herbert and I watched as they walked home on opposite sides of the street.

I went back to say good-bye to my guardian and apologize for the fight.

"Don't worry about it," Jaggers said. "I like that Spider," referring to Drummle.

"I don't," I replied.

Jaggers advised me to stay away from Drummle, even though Jaggers said that he liked Drummle.

About a month later, Spider's time at Mr. Pocket's was up. He went home to his family.

CHAPTER 13
A Visit from Joe

My Dear Mr. Pip,

I write this letter at the request of Mr. Gargery. On Tuesday, he will be in London with Mr. Wopsle. He would be most pleased if you would agree to meet with him. Your poor sister is the same. We speak of you every night. I hope you will agree to meet with Joe, even though you are now a gentleman.

Your obliged servant,
Biddy

I received Biddy's letter on the day before Joe was to arrive. I confess that

I did not look forward to Joe's visit. I feared that he might embarrass me. I was happy that he was coming to Barnard's Inn and not to Mr. Pocket's.

I cleaned up the apartment. Everything looked splendid.

"How are you, Joe?" I asked when he arrived.

"How *air* you, Pip?" he responded, trying to sound refined.

Joe told me about everyone back home. Biddy was well. Mr. Wopsle had

left the church to become an actor.

While we were catching up, Herbert came in. I introduced him to Joe. After coffee, Herbert left for work.

"Us two being alone, sir–" Joe began.

"How can you call me, sir?" I interrupted. By that time I was annoyed with Joe. He had dropped his hat several times during coffee with Herbert, and he did not speak proper English.

Although Joe was not dressed in the finest clothes, he had an air of dignity about him. I realized that he always had.

"It was not just to break vittles with gentlemen that I came," he said. "Pumblechook come into the public house the other night and was tellin' people that he had been your companion all your life."

"Nonsense," I said. "You have always been my companion."

"I hoped you'd say that," Joe said. "Pumblechook really came in to tell me that Miss Havisham wished to see me."

He had my attention now. Joe said that he went to see Miss Havisham the next day. She asked Joe to let me know that Estella was home. I could visit her if I wished.

As he rose to leave, I said, "Don't go now, Joe."

"I must," he said.

My heart sank as he shook my hand.

"Pip, dear old chap," Joe said, "life is made of so many partings welded together. One man's a blacksmith, one's a whitesmith, and one's a goldsmith. Divisions among such must come. I am sorry that we won't be seeing each other in London again. I am out of place away from the forge."

He touched me gently on the forehead, and then he walked out.

CHAPTER 14

A Reunion with Estella

Imade up my mind to return home the next day, but I decided not to stay at Joe's. I convinced myself that I would be an inconvenience. But I really wanted to stay at the Blue Boar to be closer to Miss Havisham's.

In those days, it was customary for convicts to be transported by coach. There would be two such convicts traveling with me. They were chained together at the ankles. A guard was with them. I recognized one of the convicts. He was the man from the public house who had given me the two one-pound notes!

The coach was almost ready to leave with the convicts and their guard. The convicts were to sit up front with their guard. The passenger who was to sit next to them made a fuss. He didn't want to be near them. The guard assured him that the convicts would sit opposite him and would not bother him.

"Don't blame me," growled the convict I had recognized. "I don't want to go. Anyone's welcome to my place."

At last, we were all settled into the coach and I was considering returning two one-pound notes to the man.

As I was thinking, I dozed off. To my surprise, the first words I heard uttered as I woke up were, "Two one-pound notes." The man I recognized was talking to the other convict. "As I was about to be discharged, he asked me to give two one-pound notes to the boy who had kept his secret and fed him," the convict explained. "Later, he was convicted of breaking out of prison. He's in for life."

I was sure that he did not recognize

me, but just in case, I jumped off of the coach as soon as we arrived in town.

Finally, I reached the Blue Boar. As I was eating dinner, I read a copy of the local newspaper. I was surprised to see an article about a young man who had just come into a fortune. This article mentioned a kind uncle as the boy's patron. I got the feeling that if I traveled to the farthest corner of the world, I would find someone who had heard that Pumblechook was my patron!

I woke very early in the morning.

Since it was too early to call on Miss Havisham, I decided to take a walk. My thoughts turned to Joe, and I felt guilty. I decided that I would visit Joe the next day.

I believed that Miss Havisham's intention was to bring Estella and me together. I loved Estella. I knew that I loved her against reason and hope, but I loved her anyway.

I was quite nervous when the time came for me to ring the bell. After some time, I managed to do it. I had my back to the gate and turned swiftly when I heard it creak open. The last person in the world I expected to see opened the gate. It was Orlick!

"Yes," Orlick said when he saw my surprised expression. "More lives than yours have changed." He told me that he had left Joe's forge. He was now employed by Miss Havisham to protect Satis House against criminals.

"May I see Miss Havisham?" I asked.

"How should I know?" Orlick replied.

He was as nasty as ever. I shrugged and walked past him. I went up to see Miss Havisham. She was in her chair near the old table. She still wore her old wedding dress. Beside her sat a lady that I had never seen before.

"How do you do, Pip?" Miss Havisham asked.

"I came as soon as I heard that you wanted to see me," I said.

The other lady lifted her eyes and looked at me. It was Estella! She had changed since I had last seen her. She was much more beautiful. When she held out her hand, I stammered something about my having looked forward to seeing her for a long time.

"Is he changed?" Miss Havisham asked Estella.

"Very much," said Estella, carefully looking me over.

I learned that Estella had just come back from France and that she would

soon be off to London.

Miss Havisham told us to take a walk in the garden. Estella and I obliged.

"I hid and watched your fight that day," Estella confessed. "I was quite against your opponent. I was afraid that he would be brought here to pester me."

"He and I are friends now," I told her.

"Now that your fortune has changed, you must change your companions," she said matter-of-factly.

My resolution to visit Joe vanished. Estella walked with an air of superiority. It made me feel like a young boy. I asked her if she remembered having made me cry the first day we met. She did not.

"I have no heart," she said. "I am not sentimental about such things." Her words deeply hurt me.

At last we went back into the house. I found out that my guardian had been

visiting Miss Havisham on business and would return for dinner.

Miss Havisham asked me to push her around the room in her chair, as I had done in the old days. The entire time I watched Estella, who looked more beautiful than ever. Soon Estella left the room to get ready for dinner.

When she was gone, Miss Havisham asked me if I admired Estella more than ever. I hesitated for a moment, then admitted that I did.

She drew my head close to hers. "Love

her! Love her!" she cried. "If she favors you, love her! If she tears your heart apart, love her! I raised her to be loved. Real love is giving up your heart and soul, as I did." It sounded like she was placing a curse on me.

Just then, Jaggers came into the room. I noticed that Miss Havisham appeared to be as frightened of him as everyone else was.

Miss Havisham instructed Jaggers and me to go down to dinner. On our way down, Jaggers asked me how many times I had actually dined with Miss Havisham. I told him that I never had. He told me that Miss Havisham always ate by herself, in the middle of the night. I asked Jaggers if he knew Estella's last name. It was Havisham, he said.

During dinner, I noticed that Jaggers never looked at Estella, but she often stared at him with curiosity. I wondered why, since she usually acted disinterested and bored.

After dinner, we played cards for many

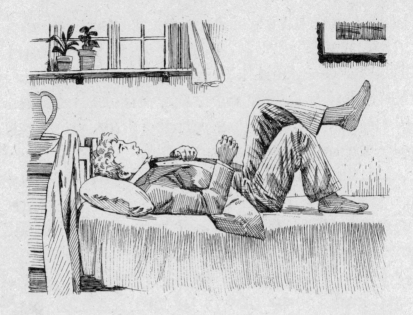

hours. Then it was time for me to leave. It was arranged that when Estella came to London, I was to meet her at the coach station.

As I lay down on my bed in my room at the Blue Boar, I felt good. It seemed as though Miss Havisham certainly intended Estella for me—a former blacksmith's boy.

CHAPTER 15

Estella Comes to London

The next morning, I told Jaggers what I knew of Orlick's past. I said that he wasn't to be trusted at Miss Havisham's. Jaggers seemed to delight in the information. He said that he would pay Orlick and relieve him of his duties.

When I got back to London, I sent Joe a barrel of oysters because I felt badly about not visiting him. Then I went straight to Barnard's Inn. I found Herbert having dinner. I decided to confide my troubles to my dear friend.

"Herbert," I said, "I love Estella."

"I knew that all along," Herbert replied.

"How?" I asked. "I never told you."

"I could tell by the way you spoke of

her," he said.

"Well, I saw her yesterday," I explained. "She is more beautiful than ever."

"It is a good thing that you were picked out for her," Herbert said. "Do you have any idea how she feels about you?" I told him that I did not. Herbert advised me to be patient and good things would come to me. He was quite a cheerful chap.

Then he proposed a dreadful thought. He told me that it was possible that Estella was not intended for me. After all, Jaggers never mentioned a marriage as a part of my arrangement. He asked if I could possibly try to forget her. I told him that was impossible.

We changed the subject. Herbert told me that soon all of his brothers and sisters were to be married. Arrangements had been made at their births. His engagement was a secret. The girl's name was Clara. She lived in London. Her father was once rich, but now he

was an invalid.

One day, while I was studying with Mr. Pocket, I received a note. Estella was to arrive in London the next day. I was to meet her coach.

My appetite vanished. I was quite nervous. I arrived at the station hours early. I didn't want to risk missing Estella's coach.

Finally, her coach arrived. In her fur-trimmed traveling clothes, Estella was even more delicately beautiful than ever. She pointed out her luggage to me so that I could pick all of it up for her.

"I am going to Richmond," she told me. "You are to take me. I have a carriage. You and I have no choice but to obey our instructions. We are not free to follow our own wills." She was going to Richmond to live with a rich lady who had many connections. She would introduce Estella to many people.

Estella and I decided to have dinner together. She put her arm through mine

as we walked into the dining room of the coach station.

After we were seated, she asked, "How are you doing at Mr. Pocket's?"

"As well as I can without being with you," I replied. I didn't want to miss the opportunity to tell her how I felt.

"You silly boy," Estella replied.

Estella told me that Mr. Pocket's family (not Mr. Pocket himself) wrote to Miss Havisham frequently. They misrepresented me and said bad things

about me. They seemed to have a hatred for me. Estella began to laugh.

"I hope that you do not find it amusing that they harm me," I said.

"No," she said. "I laugh because they fail. It gives me satisfaction to see those people thwarted. You did not have to grow up in that strange house with those people conspiring against you. I did."

Estella told me that they could not make me look bad to Miss Havisham.

She held her hand out playfully, and I kissed it. I asked if I would be permitted to kiss her cheek. She let me. But as soon as I kissed her, she got up and acted very businesslike.

We finished our tea and boarded the coach to Richmond. We passed the prison on our way. Estella seemed disgusted by it. I told her that Jaggers knew more secrets about that place than any man in London.

"He knows secrets about many places," Estella murmured.

"Do you see him often?" I asked.

"I see him on occasion," Estella answered. "I have since I was young. But I don't know much about him."

As we drove along, I pointed out all of the interesting places in London. Before her trip to France, Estella had never left Miss Havisham's neighborhood.

Estella informed me that I was to visit her often in Richmond. She told me that I had been mentioned to the family that she was to live with. It was a mother and her daughter.

We reached Richmond all too soon. As I watched Estella enter the house, I thought of how happy I would be if I married her. But I also thought that I was never happy when I was with her. In fact, she made me feel miserable.

CHAPTER 16
A Death in the Family

By this time, I had grown accustomed to my great expectations. They had an effect on my character. I was always sad because of the way I had treated Joe. Sometimes I thought that I would be happier if I had never met Miss Havisham but had grown up to be a blacksmith.

My extravagant ways led Herbert to spend money that he couldn't afford. I had disrupted the simplicity of his life. I had filled his apartment with lavish furniture. I would have taken Herbert's expenses on myself, but he was proud and would not allow me. Before long, my own debt began to grow, as did Herbert's.

Clearly we were headed for ruin.

At Startop's suggestion, we joined a group called Finches of the Grove. The Finches spent their money foolishly. We ate at a very fancy restaurant once every two weeks.

Sometimes I would say, "My dear Herbert, we are getting on badly."

"My dear Handel," Herbert would say, "I was about to say the same thing."

Then we would order a fine dinner and sit down to settle our debts by writing down all of our expenses. As we were doing so one night, a letter arrived for me. Its contents simply told me that my sister had passed away. I was expected home the next day.

It was the first time that someone in my life I could remember had died. The thought of my sister sitting in her chair in the kitchen haunted me. I recalled my sister with tenderness. I wished that I had better avenged her attack many years ago.

When I arrived home for the funeral, I found many people there. Poor Joe sat alone in the corner of the room. He clasped my hand when I came in. Biddy, wearing a modest black dress, was very helpful. Pumblechook was also there, stuffing his face. All he talked about was my fortune.

We all walked to the cemetery. My sister was laid quietly into the earth.

When everyone had finally gone home, Biddy, Joe and I sat down to a

quiet dinner. Afterward, I went for a walk with Biddy. I asked her why she hadn't written to me sooner about my sister's state. Biddy said that she didn't think I would want to be bothered.

Now that my sister had died, Biddy was going to move out to live with the Hubbles. She said that she hoped she would still be able to take care of Joe in some way. She was worried about him.

"How are you going to live, Biddy?" I asked. "Do you want any money?"

Biddy would hear nothing of me giving her money. She was going to try to get a teaching job.

I asked Biddy to tell me exactly how my sister had died. She told me that Mrs. Joe asked her to place her arms around Joe's neck. My sister, who had not said a word in years, then said the words "Joe," "pardon," and "Pip." Then she was gone. Biddy cried as she told the story. Nothing was ever discovered about my sister's attacker.

"What has become of Orlick?" I asked.

"He works in the quarries," Biddy told me. She tried to tell me that she had not seen him lately. But I knew she was lying. He was still following her. It made me angry to know that he still pursued her.

To change the subject, she told me how much Joe loved me and that he never complained. I knew she was talking about how I had ignored Joe. I told Biddy that I would visit often. I wouldn't leave poor Joe alone. I don't think that Biddy believed me, though. Her disbelief hurt me deeply.

Early the next morning, I stood at the forge window looking at Joe. Then I went in and bid him farewell. I told him I would be back often.

"Never too soon and never too often," Joe said.

I am afraid, though, that Biddy was right about my not coming back often.

CHAPTER 17

Drummle's New Love

Herbert turned twenty-one eight months before I did. There was little fuss made about it at Barnard's Inn. But we had something to look forward to on my birthday. We thought that Jaggers would make an announcement about my fortune. Wemmick called me to the office. I was sure that something great would happen.

When I arrived at the office, Wemmick congratulated me. I went in immediately to see Jaggers and receive the news.

Jaggers told me that the identity of my benefactor would not be revealed to me today. He only told me that it could possibly be years before that happened. He

commented on the large sums of money I had been spending. I was to receive five hundred pounds per year until the day I met my benefactor. He did not know anything of my future with Estella.

A few days later, I paid a visit to the Castle. Wemmick was just returning from a walk. A woman named Miss Skiffins was with him. I learned that she was a frequent visitor at the Castle.

I took a walk with Wemmick. After thinking for a long time, I asked him to help me find a way to help Herbert. I wanted some of the money from my fortune to be transferred to him. I wanted this to happen without Herbert knowing it. He would certainly not accept it if he knew the source.

Wemmick said that Miss Skiffins's brother, who was an accountant, might be able to help me. He would inquire.

We rejoined Miss Skiffins and the Aged for tea. Wemmick and Miss Skiffins sat next to each other, and I noticed that Wemmick tried to put his arm around her shoulder. Miss Skiffins promptly removed it. This went on for some time before I decided to leave.

After a week had passed, Wemmick told me that he had found a solution to my problem. Miss Skiffins's brother located a young merchant, Clarriker, who was in search of an intelligent helper. I secretly paid Clarriker cash, in Herbert's name, and the deal was done. As agreed upon, Clarriker called on Herbert and offered him the job.

Herbert was more than happy to accept the proposal, and he knew nothing of my involvement.

Meanwhile, I often visited Estella in Richmond. She was living with a woman named Mrs. Brandley and her daughter, who was a few years older than Estella. Estella had many admirers.

"Miss Havisham wishes me to return to Satis House for the day," Estella informed me. "You are to take me." She smiled her cold smile that always chilled me.

When we arrived, Miss Havisham doted on Estella as she had always done. She took pleasure in finding out all of the ways in which Estella abused me. I realized then that Miss Havisham wanted Estella to wreak havoc on men as revenge on her behalf. She had hated men ever since her fiancé abandoned her.

Miss Havisham and Estella were sitting together next to the fire. When Estella stood, Miss Havisham asked if

Estella was tired of her already. Without waiting for an answer, Miss Havisham said that Estella was ungrateful. Estella just stared coldly at her benefactor.

"Have you nothing to say, you cold girl?" Miss Havisham yelled.

"How dare you, of all people, call me cold?" Estella replied. "You have made me what I am today."

A harsh, bitter fight followed. Miss Havisham accused Estella of being hard-hearted. Estella accused Miss Havisham

of raising her to be so. After much yelling, we all retired to bed.

A few days later, there was a meeting of the Finches. It was customary for a different member each week to pledge his love for a lady. This week it was dull Drummle's turn.

When asked to name the object of his affection, Drummle stated," Estella."

Imagine my surprise and disappointment! I asked him to tell us which Estella he spoke of. He said he spoke of Estella from Richmond. I refused to believe that my Estella could be interested in dull, grumpy Drummle. But he produced a note, in Estella's handwriting, stating that she had the pleasure of dancing with him several times.

I would have been miserable to learn that Estella favored anyone but me. I was doubly hurt and angry because it was Drummle. Apparently, Drummle had been pursuing Estella for some time. He had been waiting for just the right moment to reveal his intentions. He knew that Estella would see his family's money as an asset.

A ball was held a few days later in Richmond, and the Finches attended. Drummle spent the entire evening dancing with Estella.

"Why do you let him hang all over you?" I asked Estella.

"I cannot help it if he is attracted to me," Estella replied.

"You know that he is not a good person," I said. "All he has is money. Why would you spend time with him?"

"I am merely deceiving and entrapping him," she said. "I do that to all men, except you." That was all she would say about the matter.

She was hurting me more than she would ever know.

CHAPTER 18

The Truth Revealed

My twenty-third birthday had just passed, but I heard not another word about my expectations. Herbert and I had moved out of Barnard's Inn. We lived in Temple, down by the river. Although I had finished my studies with Mr. Pocket, I still visited him.

One night when Herbert was away I looked out my window and saw a man looking up.

"What floor do you want?" I asked.

"Top floor. I want to see Mr. Pip," he said. I told him to come up.

The man was muscular and looked to be about sixty years old. He seemed pleased to see me.

"I will explain my business, Master," he said. He looked around with a strange sense of pleasure. He told me that he needed a minute to soak it all in. I thought he was disturbed.

Then suddenly I realized that he was my convict from the marshes!

"You were noble back then," he said. "I'll never forget what you did for me."

"How have you been?" I asked. He told me that he had done many different things over the years and he had done very well for himself.

I told him that the man he had sent long ago gave me the two one-pound notes, just as he had instructed. I said that I wanted to pay him back now. He wouldn't take the money.

"May I make a guess about your fortune?" he asked. "You receive five hundred pounds a year. And you have a guardian. His name begins with a J."

So he had been my benefactor all along—not Miss Havisham! He had done it to thank me for helping him all those years ago. Estella had never been part of the plan, after all. I wished I had never met him. Then I would still be at the forge and I would be happy. I would never have had such expectations.

Since Estella was not intended for me, it made me even more miserable that I had deserted Joe for no reason at all. I knew that I could never undo what I had done.

My dreaded visitor stayed the night. Although I was grateful for what he had done, I was a bit afraid of him—he being a convict. I had to hide him because there were people on his trail.

I went downstairs to ask the watchman for a lantern. On my way down, I stumbled over a man at the bottom of the staircase. He did not answer when I called to him. When I came back with the watchman, he was gone. I checked my apartment. It seemed odd that on that night of all nights, with my convict in the house, a strange man would be on the stairs.

I asked the watchman if he had seen any strange men.

"A strange man called for you," he said. "Did you see him?"

"Yes, that was my uncle," I lied.

"Did you see the person with him?" he asked.

I told him that I had not seen a second person.

He told me that the man went the other way when my convict came to my apartment. He was wearing a dark coat and dust-covered clothes.

With nothing else to do, I went to sleep. When I awoke in the morning, I waited for my convict to wake up. Finally, he came out of Herbert's room, where he had slept. I asked him what his name was.

"My assumed name is Provis," he said. "My real name is Abel Magwitch." From then on, I called him Mr. Provis.

"Was there anyone with you last night?" I asked.

"No," he answered. "Pip, it makes me proud to see what I've made you."

I ignored his comment. "How will you be kept out of danger? How long will you remain here?" I asked.

"I'm here to stay," he said. "I'll wear a disguise so the police don't find me."

I went out to buy new clothes for him and a wig to hide his true identity. I decided to pay a visit to Jaggers. I could tell as soon as I saw him that he knew Provis had come back.

"Don't tell me anything," Jaggers said. "I don't want to know anything."

"A man named Magwitch told me that he was my benefactor," I said. "Is it true? Was it only he?"

"He alone," Jaggers answered.

"All along I was sure that it was Miss Havisham," I said.

"I never led you to believe that," Jaggers said coldly. "Magwitch always insisted that I stick to the facts."

Jaggers said to pretend that Magwitch was in South Wales. He said that if Magwitch was found back in the country, he would be executed. That was the rule of his sentence. Since there was no more that Jaggers could tell me, I left.

The next day, Provis's new clothes arrived. No matter what he put on, he still looked like a convict. I hated that he was staying with me. Finally, on the fifth day, Herbert cheerfully came bursting through the door, back from his visit to France.

Herbert was astonished to find Provis in the apartment. I introduced them, but Herbert had no idea who Provis really was. I was anxious for Provis to go to bed. Finally, when Provis had retired, I told Herbert the whole story.

"The truth is that I am attached to this dreadful man," I concluded.

"My poor Handel," Herbert said.

"Think of all that I owe him already," I complained. "And he wants to give me more. The truth is that I have no expectations now. My benefactor is a criminal. I am fit for nothing."

"Don't say fit for nothing," Herbert said. "Clarriker can give you a position. I am on my way to becoming his partner, you know." Poor Herbert—he had no idea where the funding had come from.

Herbert and I discussed how angry Provis would be if I broke away from him. He was a dangerous man. Yet, we had to get him out of England. After all, the prison was only a block away from our apartment.

CHAPTER 19
More Revelations

The next morning, Provis told us his life story. He said that he was born an orphan and had grown up to be a scoundrel. He was constantly in and out of jail for various crimes.

When he met a man named Compeyson, he became Compeyson's partner in crime. They were thieves and forgers. Compeyson had a friend named Arthur. Years before, Compeyson and Arthur swindled a woman out of a lot of money. Then they had foolishly wasted the money. Arthur died soon after Provis met Compeyson.

Provis and Compeyson were convicted of felony. Provis was sentenced to fourteen years in prison. Compeyson was sentenced to seven years. The judge had mercy on him because he had been a gentleman.

Provis hated Compeyson for that. One day in jail, Provis hit Compeyson in the face and escaped the prison. Compeyson followed. That was when I first met him. Provis never heard from Compeyson again.

Herbert scribbled some words on a piece of paper. The note informed me

that Miss Havisham's half-brother's name was Arthur. So Compeyson was the man who had left Miss Havisham on their wedding day!

I decided to go to Richmond to visit Estella the next day. When I arrived at Mrs. Brandley's house, I learned that Estella had gone to Satis House.

So I went to Satis House. Herbert said he would look after Provis for the one evening that I would be gone.

When I arrived at the Blue Boar, I was shocked to see Drummle there. We pretended not to notice each other. After a while, I couldn't help myself, and I made myself known to Drummle. He told me that he was to dine with Estella that evening. I couldn't have been angrier.

Drummle went outside to mount his horse. A man in dust-covered clothes lit his cigar for him. The man reminded me of Orlick.

At Satis House, I found Miss

Havisham sitting next to the fire. Estella was seated at her feet, knitting.

I told them that I had discovered the identity of my patron and that he would not enrich my station in life.

"It was pure coincidence that Mr. Jaggers was my lawyer as well as your patron's," said Miss Havisham.

"Why did you let me believe that you were my patron and that you intended me for Estella?" I asked sadly. "That wasn't kind."

"I never pretended to be kind," Miss Havisham said.

I told Miss Havisham that Mr. Pocket and Herbert were good people. They were not like the rest of their family. I asked Miss Havisham, as a favor, to finish paying Clarriker for Herbert's partnership. I told her that it must be done in secret. Surely, I said, I could not continue to take money from Provis to do the service. Miss Havisham did not answer.

I turned to Estella. "Estella, you know

that I love you," I said. "I should have said it sooner." Estella looked unmoved by my words. Miss Havisham looked from me to Estella and then back again.

"I know that I have no hope that I will ever call you mine," I continued. "My future is uncertain. Yet, I have loved you since the day I first saw you. It was cruel of Miss Havisham to play upon the feelings of a small boy and torture me for all of these years." I saw Miss Havisham put her hand on her heart.

"I do not understand your feelings," Estella said calmly. "You stir no feelings in me. I tried to warn you of this. This is my nature."

"I know that I can't be with you," I said. "But please don't let Drummle pursue you. You cannot love him."

"I am going to marry him," she said.

"Don't let Miss Havisham lead you into doing this," I begged.

"It is my own decision," Estella said.

I took her hand, and my bitter tears touched her skin. She told me that my feelings for her would pass. I told her that would never happen. She was a part of me and always would be.

I decided to return home earlier than expected. When I arrived at the gate, the watchman handed me a note. It was from Wemmick. It read: DO NOT GO HOME!

CHAPTER 20

Estella's Parents

Heeding the warning, I went imme-diately to Covent Garden and secured a hotel room.

It was a terrible night with no sleep. Wemmick's note kept flashing through my mind. What would I find when I finally did go home?

The next morning, I went to Wemmick's house. He told me that a certain convict I knew had caused quite a stir. My house was being watched. From what Wemmick told me, I knew that the person watching my house was Compeyson. Wemmick had told Herbert to get Provis out of the apartment right away, so Herbert had hidden him at Clara's house.

I went to Clara's house immediately. Herbert told me that Provis was in a bedroom upstairs.

I told them about how Compeyson was looking for Provis and that Wemmick had suggested that we stay out of sight.

Herbert suggested that he and I row Provis down the river in the middle of the night. I liked this scheme, and Provis was quite elated by it. We would row up and down the river every night for days or weeks. Then when we carried Provis off, no one would notice us.

Meanwhile, I was being pressed by creditors to pay my debts. Yet, I refused to take more money from Provis. It was an unhappy life I now led.

A few weeks later, I ran into Jaggers. He insisted that I dine with him and Wemmick. During dinner, Jaggers gave me a note from Miss Havisham. She requested that I go to Satis House. She wanted to discuss the matter of Herbert's partnership.

Jaggers employed a housekeeper named Molly. On this night, I noticed that Molly had the same hands as Estella. When I looked at her face, I noticed that she had Estella's eyes, as well. I was sure that this woman must be Estella's birth mother.

As Wemmick and I walked home, I asked what he knew about Molly. He said that she had been tried for murder and acquitted. While she was on trial, she had to give up her daughter. Since the trial, she had had been employed by Jaggers.

I went to visit Miss Havisham the next day. I sat down beside her and she said, "Perhaps you can never believe that I have a heart," she said. "But I would like to do what I can to help."

I explained the secret partnership to her. She asked if I could forgive her for what she had done to me. To my amazement, she dropped to her knees.

"What have I done!" she cried. I asked her if Estella married Drummle. She said, "Yes."

"I didn't realize the depth of the damage I had done," she continued, "until you confessed your love for Estella." She said she now knew that she had damaged Estella's heart.

I asked her to tell me how she had come to adopt Estella. She said that Jaggers had brought the little girl to her when Estella had been about three years old. I was now convinced that Molly was Estella's mother. Miss Havisham was quite distraught, so I decided to leave. First I walked all around the building, somehow sensing that I would not see it again.

Suddenly I had a feeling that something bad had happened to Miss Havisham, so I went back to check. When I entered the room, Miss Havisham came running toward me in a blaze of fire. In her anguish, she had fallen into the fireplace. Quickly, I put out the flames.

I did my best to comfort her while

we waited for the doctor to arrive. The doctor came at once. Miss Havisham had serious injuries. Estella was in Paris. The doctor said he would write to her right away.

Before I left, I told Miss Havisham that I had forgiven her.

My hands and arms were badly burned from trying to save her. When I got home, Herbert devoted a whole day to taking care of me.

Herbert had spent a lot of time with Provis during the last few weeks. Provis had revealed a shocking secret to my dear friend.

A long time ago, Provis was married. His wife had been accused of murder, but was acquitted. The wife had had to give their little girl away. The woman had led Provis to believe that the little girl had died. This all happened about four years before I met Provis.

"The man we have in hiding is Estella's father!" I exclaimed.

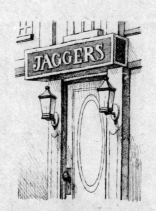

CHAPTER 21

Danger for Pip

I decided to visit Jaggers the next morning. I wanted to get the full truth from him.

"I know the identity of Estella's birth mother," I reported.

Jaggers looked quite shocked. "Her mother?" he repeated.

"Perhaps I know more of Estella's history than even you do," I said. "I know her father, too."

"So! You know the young lady's father, Pip?" Mr. Jaggers asked.

"Yes," I replied. "It's Provis."

Then I told Jaggers and Wemmick all that I knew. I was careful not to mention Wemmick's part in providing me

with some of the information.

Jaggers told me that he had left Estella with Miss Havisham for her own good. With her mother on trial, Estella's life was in danger. It would do no one involved any good to reveal the secret.

Before I left, Jaggers gave me Miss Havisham's check for Herbert's partnership. When I delivered it, Clarriker said that the business was prospering. Herbert would do well in the future.

Herbert and I decided to ask Startop to help us with Provis's escape, but we would tell him as little as possible. Once we had rowed Provis down the river, we would board a steamer to Hamburg, Germany.

On the day before the escape, I found a letter at my door. It directed me to go alone to the marshes that night. There, I would receive information about my "Uncle Provis."

I left immediately. On my way to the marshes, I stopped at Satis House to ask about Miss Havisham. She was still in great pain.

When I reached the Blue Boar, I overheard the man at the desk talking about a young boy whom Pumblechook had brought into fortune. I asked him if he knew the young man. He did not.

"Is Pumblechook the only person to whom this young man is grateful?" I asked the man.

"Yes. Pumblechook did everything for him," he answered.

This made my heart ache for Joe and Biddy. Joe had done so much for me, yet he never took credit for it.

With no time to spare, I headed for the marshes. It was a dark night. Rain had started to fall. Suddenly, I was grabbed from behind. The force hurt my burned arm as I tried to struggle.

"Now I've got you," said a mean voice.

"Help!" I cried.

It was Orlick! He was angry that I had caused him to lose his job at Miss

Havisham's all those years ago. But that was not all.

"How dare you come between me and a young woman I liked?" he barked. He was speaking of Biddy and the warnings I gave her about him.

I thought about what would happen if Orlick killed me. Provis would think I had deserted him. Herbert would doubt me. Joe and Biddy would never know that I was sorry for the way I had treated them.

"I was your sister's attacker," Orlick

confessed. "I did it to hurt you. And it was me you stumbled over on your stairs that night."

I yelled and kicked Orlick. Suddenly I heard voices and saw two men struggling with Orlick. I looked up to see that my savior was Herbert. Orlick ran off.

"Herbert! And Startop!" I yelled.

"Easy, Handel," Herbert said. He helped me up.

In my hurry, I had dropped Orlick's note. Herbert found it and recruited Startop to find me. They took me back to London and tended my wounds.

CHAPTER 22
A Foiled Escape

The next day we put our plan to help
Provis into action. Herbert, Startop,
Provis, and I rowed down the river. We
planned to board the first steamer that
came past us. Provis thanked me again
and again.

"If all goes well," I said, "you will be
free and safe within a few hours."

"I hope so," Provis replied.

After many hours of rowing, we docked
the boat and went ashore. We found
lodgings for the night. I slept well for a
few hours. Then I looked out the window
and saw two men looking into our boat.
They quickly fled across the marshes.

The next morning I told my companions what I had seen. Provis, as usual,

didn't seem worried. So we again set off down the river.

Finally, we were in the path of a steamer that was headed for Hamburg. As there was another steamer coming quickly behind us, Provis and I got ready to board the first steamer. We said our good-byes to Herbert and Startop.

But before we could board the steamer, another boat came up beside us. The crew was after Provis and wanted him to surrender.

Provis leaned across to the other boat and pulled the cloak off of a passenger. It was Compeyson! Before I knew it, Provis and Compeyson had both gone into the water, and our boat had capsized. I was saved and taken on board the boat Compeyson had been on. Herbert and Startop were there, too, but the two convicts were gone.

Finally, we spotted Provis swimming in the cold water. He was taken on board and handcuffed. He told us that

he and Compeyson had struggled underwater. He freed himself, but Compeyson had drowned.

Now that "My Uncle Provis" had been taken by the police, he was called from then on by his real name, Magwitch. The next day, Magwitch and I left for London. Once again, we bid Herbert and Startop farewell.

My disgust for Magwitch had melted away. Now that he was a shackled prisoner again, I felt bad. I saw him as a man who only wished to help me by being my benefactor.

I told Magwitch that I felt guilty. He had come back to London to see me, and now he was a prisoner.

"I'm content to take my chances," Magwitch said. "I've seen my boy, and he can be a gentleman without me."

When Compeyson's body was found, several notes were discovered in a case he had in his pocket. One of the notes listed the name of a bank where Magwitch had a large sum of money. Compeyson had hoped to gain a reward by turning in Magwitch, no doubt.

Soon after Magwitch's capture, I received more bad news from Herbert.

"My dear Handel, I shall soon have to leave you, just when you most need me," Herbert told me. His new partnership was going to take him to Cairo, in Egypt.

"Herbert, I shall always need you, because you are my best friend," I said. "But this is a wonderful opportunity for you. Don't worry about me."

Still, Herbert was worried about my

future. He offered me a job as a clerk with his company. Herbert wanted me to move with him and Clara to Cairo. I told him that I might join them in six months.

At the end of the week, I saw Herbert off. I ran into Wemmick as I left the station. He asked me to come to the Castle the next morning.

At the Castle, he asked me to take a walk with him. We passed a church. Wemmick casually asked me to go inside with him.

When we stepped into the church, I realized the real reason for my being there. Wemmick was going to marry Miss Skiffins! I was the best man. It was a lovely wedding.

CHAPTER 23

Sorrow and
Joy

Magwitch remained very ill in prison. He had broken his ribs and was very badly bruised. I had the chance to visit with him every day, but for a short time only. His condition worsened with each day that passed.

After about a month, the time arrived for Magwitch's trial. The judge and jury found him guilty and sentenced him to death.

I hoped that he would die of his injuries before being put to death in a humiliating way. I wrote a petition to the court. I reported all that Magwitch had done for me and that he had come back to England for me.

While we awaited final word, I visited Magwitch every day.

"Thank you, dear boy," Magwitch said on one such visit. "You never deserted me."

I pressed his hand in silence. I could not forget that I had once meant to desert him. He had great difficulty breathing. I took this opportunity to tell him about Estella, before time ran out.

"Your daughter lived. She is living now," I said. "She is a very beautiful lady and I love her!"

He raised my hands to his lips, and then Magwitch passed away.

After Magwitch died, I was alone. I would come home day after day and go to sleep. I had many debts and no money to pay them.

Soon, I became very ill. I had a high fever. Later, I was told that I slipped in and out of consciousness for almost a month. When I finally awoke, my faithful friend Joe was sitting at my side.

Joe laid his head down on the pillow at my side and hugged me. He was overjoyed that I recognized him. I felt so ashamed at how I abandoned him, and how I had wanted to be smarter then he was.

"Joe, you break my heart," I cried. "Don't be nice to me. I was so cruel to you, I wish you would be angry at me."

"Pip, you and me has always been friends," Joe said. He wiped tears from his eyes. Joe stayed by my side for

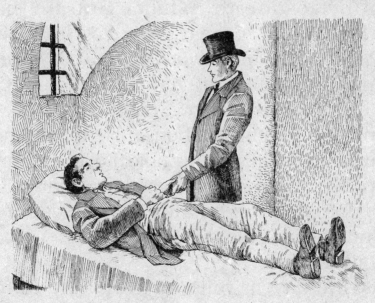

more than a month while I was ill. He also paid all of my debts.

Biddy had encouraged Joe to come to me when word of my illness reached them. Joe sat down to write a letter to Biddy to let her know that I was now well. Biddy had taught Joe how to write!

When I asked Joe about Miss Havisham, he told me that she had passed away shortly after the accident in which she was burned. She left most of her estate to Estella. But she had also left a great sum to Matthew Pocket. My kind words about Matthew must have encouraged her to do so.

He told me that one night, Orlick broke into Pumblechook's house. He robbed him and beat him up. Pumblechook was able to identify him. Orlick was now in jail.

Joe took me for rides in the country. He looked after me and took care of me for months.

One day, I woke up early and found

a note from Joe. Now that I needed him no longer, he had gone home.

I decided to go back home to Joe's. I wanted to apologize to him and Biddy. I would also ask her if she could ever love me. She was a good person. I admired her. I planned to ask her to marry me.

The next day, I went to the forge. After walking around town for some time, I decided it was time to talk to Joe and Biddy. I expected to hear Joe's hammer clinking, but the forge was quiet. I went up to the house. There were many people in the parlor.

"It's my wedding day," cried Biddy happily. "I am married to Joe!"

"Dear Biddy," I said, "you have the best husband in the whole world! And Joe, you have the best wife a man could want." I was truly happy that they were both so happy. They, above all others, deserved true happiness.

CHAPTER 24
A New Expectation

I told Biddy and Joe that I planned to go to Cairo and work with Herbert. I wanted to pay them back. I was overjoyed that they had both forgiven me for acting so cruelly toward them.

Within a month, I left England and joined Herbert in Cairo. In a year's time, I had become a partner. When Clarriker told Herbert about how his partnership had been funded, Herbert was touched.

After living happily with Herbert and his wife, Clara, for eleven years, I went home and visited Joe. I walked into the kitchen and found him sitting near the fire with a little boy—his son.

"We named him Pip," Joe said, "in

honor of you." Joe and Biddy also had a daughter.

One day, Biddy asked me if I still loved Estella. I told her that I did, but that I had settled quite nicely for a bachelor's life.

I learned that Estella had been in an unhappy marriage. Drummle had treated her cruelly. He had died some years ago. I didn't have any idea what had become of her since then.

I visited the remains of Satis House

the next day. The house was gone. All that remained was the garden wall. I spotted a solitary figure in the mist.

"Estella!" I cried.

We sat down on a bench to talk. This was the first time she had been back to Satis House in many years, she added.

"I often think of you," she said.

"You have always had a place in my heart," I answered.

I took her hand in mine as we left the ruined place. Just as the morning mists had risen long ago when I first left the forge, the evening mists were rising now. I knew that Estella and I would never again part.

About the Author

Charles Dickens was born in Landport, Hampshire, England, in 1812. He was the second of eight children.

When Dickens was very young, his father was imprisoned for debt. At the age of twelve, Dickens went to work at a shoe-polish factory. Later he served as a clerk for various law firms and worked as a court reporter for the English Parliament.

Many of his articles were published, but Dickens did not achieve popular acclaim until 1836, when he wrote his first novel, *The Pickwick Papers*.

In addition to *Great Expectations*, Dickens wrote *David Copperfield*, *A Christmas Carol*, *A Tale of Two Cities*, and many other beloved classics.

Charles Dickens died in Chatham, Kent, England, in 1870.

Treasury of Illustrated Classics